No, Yellowbelly was just terrible at being a pirate. So much so that all the other pirates laughed at him and stole his treasure.

Early one morning,
following a heavy storm,
Yellowbelly was busy mopping his deck
when a seagull squawked overhead and...

The Yellow Curse

Smack!

A great big poo landed right
in Yellowbelly's eye!

This made Yellowbelly a little cross.

He marched off to wash the poo out of his eye, but...

Whoops!

He didn't see his wooden cleaning bucket...

...and stepped right into it!

So not only did Yellowbelly have poo in his eye,
but now he also had a bucket
stuck on his foot.

If Yellowbelly had been a little cross before, now he was quite angry. He clunked into his cabin to wash his eye and put on an eye patch, but...

Whoops!

He put it on the wrong eye...

...and tumbled head over heels into his wardrobe!

So not only did Yellowbelly have poo in his eye, and a bucket stuck on his foot, but now he also had a coat hanger wedged up his sleeve.

If Yellowbelly had been quite angry before,
now he was really mad.
He dragged himself out of his wardrobe, but...

Whoops!

He didn't see his parrot's cage above him...

...and he caught the coat hanger in the door.
The door flew wide open waking up
his parrot from its snooze.

So not only did Yellowbelly have poo in his eye,
and a bucket stuck on his foot,
and a coat hanger wedged up his sleeve,
but now he also had an upset
parrot pecking at his head.

If Yellowbelly had been really mad before,

now he was absolutely furious.

He hobbled onto deck to sort himself out, but...

Whoops!

He had forgotten about his mop...

...and stepped right on the handle,
flicking a thick clump of stinky,
slimy seaweed towards him.

So not only did Yellowbelly
have poo in his eye,
and a bucket stuck on his foot,
and a coat hanger wedged up
his sleeve and an upset parrot
pecking at his head, but...

...now he also had a huge
clump of stinky, slimy seaweed
stuck to his chin!

In the chaos, Yellowbelly didn't notice that Redbeard, the meanest, scariest pirate on all the seven seas, had climbed aboard his ship!

Redbeard had come to steal Yellowbelly's treasure.
He was expecting to be met by the usual,
wimpy, cowardly Yellowbelly.

But, instead,
staggering towards
Redbeard came...

...a terrible pirate!

(With a thick wooden stump for a leg, a crooked eye patch, a hook for a hand, a crazy parrot perched on his shoulder and a slimy, straggly beard.)

"Arrrgh!"

Now Redbeard had come face-to-face with many a frightening foe in his time but this beast was, without a doubt, the ugliest, scariest, most terrible pirate he'd ever had the misfortune of sailing across!

The Yellow Curse

He did something he had never done before...

Redbeard took one look
at the plank, ran along it,
and jumped off!

From that day on,
Captain Yellowbelly was known as
'The Terrible Pirate'.

And do you know what? Nobody ever
troubled him or his treasure again.

Although he did let his parrot perch on his shoulder,
and he always kept an eye patch, a bucket,
a clump of seaweed and a coat hanger handy.

Well, you never know who might turn up uninvited!

For Archie,
the irate pirate, and Mels,
the captain's mate.

P.R.

For my two little pirates,
Mara and Luna

L.T.

First published in 2007
by Meadowside Children's Books
185 Fleet Street London EC4A 2HS
www.meadowsidebooks.com

Text © Preston Rutt 2007 · Illustrations © Leo Timmers 2007
The rights of Preston Rutt and Leo Timmers to be identified
as the author and illustrator of this work have been asserted
by them in accordance with the Copyright,
Designs and Patents Act, 1988

A CIP catalogue record for this book
is available from the British Library
10 9 8 7 6 5 4 3
Printed in China